Coinkeeper

The Avery Chronicles

Book 3

By Teresa Schapansky

Coinkeeper
The Avery Chronicles
Copyright © 2021
TNT BOOK PUBLISHING
All rights reserved.

The author may be reached at:
www.teresaschapansky.com
ISBN: 978-1-988024-12-7

DEDICATION

This book is dedicated to all kids between the ages of 0 to 99 that are looking for a quick, entertaining, and perhaps slightly educational, story.

TABLE OF CONTENTS

ACKNOWLEDGMENTS

Most sincere gratitude and appreciation to the following, for their kind assistance and very generous contributions for the purpose of this book:

723 Umayyad gold dinar
to www.coinsweekly.com for the historical information

The Umayyads
to islamichistory.org for the historical information

The Red Ghost
to Marshall Trimble, author and Official Arizona State Historian for the historical information and image

i

Coinkeeper

The Avery Chronicles

Book 3

By Teresa Schapansky

BOOK 3

Grandpa told me to meet him behind the shed, and to get there long before dark.

Well, that sounded like a lot more fun than doing homework would be, so I ran over right after school.

Grandpa was sitting on a stump under the apple tree, and he pointed at another stump across from him. I set my backpack down, and took a seat.

"These here are seed potatoes, Avery." He passed me a huge metal bowl full of potatoes, and a knife. He had his own huge bowl and knife in front of him.

"We slice these about in half, but make sure each half has at least two eyes on it." Wait, what?

"Grandpa.   Everybody knows potatoes don't have eyes." He laughed at me.

"The little green things poking out, tell us that these are sprouting, and those sprouts are called, eyes.

The more eyes on your seed potato, the more potatoes you'll get. But if you plant a seed potato with just two eyes, you'll get fewer potatoes, but they'll be bigger."

I didn't know how we would deal with all of those potatoes; there were so many. We sat there like that, cutting our potatoes and tossing the halves into a barrel.

"Once they sit for a while, the cut side will form a bit of a hard skin. They'll be ready to put in the ground then, and the ground should be warm enough for planting."

Secretly, I had begun to wonder if I should have just gone home to do my homework, after all.

My fingers were feeling pretty soggy from cutting all those potatoes.

I quickly changed my mind when grandpa began telling me a story.

"The first time I met Henry, I started calling him the Kid. He was a few years younger than me, so he didn't mind.

I had pulled the 723 Umayyad gold dinar and appeared in Silver City, New Mexico in the fall of 1874. This period of time is known as the Wild West."

"Wait, grandpa. Did you say it was a 723 coin? They made coins all the way back in the year 723?" Grandpa's eyes lit up.

"Good question, Avery. All of my

experiences led me to wonder about the same thing. So, while I've been home, I've studied coins now and then.

Did you know, the first known coins began circulating in ancient Greece in about the year 600? But that's not important now.

Back to Silver City and the Kid. Silver City was a fairly new town when I appeared. The sidewalks were made of wood and the streets were made of dirt.

I soon came to learn that the timing of my appearance was good – the fall days were not unbearably warm, and the nights were cool.

I'd heard that the summer before, had been uncomfortably hot.

I found a job on a ranch looking after cattle. It was really hard work and long days.

My hands blistered and hurt, but once they toughened up and formed callouses, it wasn't so bad.

I spent the first while feeding the calves and mucking out the pens with a pitchfork.

My boss liked my work ethic and it wasn't long before I worked my way up the ranks.

You see, Avery, everybody starts at the bottom; no matter what kind of job it is.

The ranch job paid seventy cents a day, but once I got some experience, I worked my way up to over a whole dollar a day.

I was taught how to handle a horse, and lasso the cattle.

I sure enjoyed swinging that rope and making it whistle through the air, Avery. One day I'll teach you.

The bunkhouse at the ranch was full, so I couldn't stay there.

My boss planned to expand the

bunkhouse one day, but that didn't happen during my time in Silver City.

I found a room to rent at a boarding house in town for two dollars a month.

There was no plumbing, but I was grateful for the outhouse in the backyard."

How horrifying. I had to use an outhouse once, during a school field trip. I didn't like it very much.

"Grandpa, if there was no plumbing, how did you wash or take a bath?"

Grandpa tossed another potato into the barrel, and grabbed another one to cut.

"There was a big old tub set up outside for bathing. Just for washing up, we used a porcelain basin in the hallway outside of our rooms.

I soon learned that the early bird gets the worm."

"What does that mean?" What did birds have to do with cleaning yourself, I wondered.

"Well Avery, the first one up and at'em in the morning, had use of the cleanest water.

I made darn sure I was always the first one up." I cringed.

"So, the Kid also had a room there, and that's how we first met and became instant friends.

The Kid was only about fourteen, and he had a rough start in life.

His mom got sick and died the year before. Then his stepdad just up and left Henry and his brother.

I don't know what became of his brother, but the Kid turned to the dark side. He was pretty adventurous, and that was exciting to me.

Speaking of adventure, the Kid said to me one day, "My friend, you work too hard. Life can't be all about work and no play."

I couldn't argue with him, and I was owed a few days off.

We put on our cowboy hats, chaps, and spurs, filled our canteens, saddled our horses and headed for the hills."

"What hills? What do you mean, grandpa?"

"Just the mountains, the forest, good old-fashioned trail riding. What else were two young men supposed to do for fun, back then? You tell me."

I shrugged my shoulders, because I couldn't think of a single thing.

"The Kid didn't tell me anything about his plans, but he was kind of like that, so I didn't mind.

We camped in the trees for the first two nights and slept under the stars. It was so quiet and peaceful.

Finally, on the second morning, I asked him, "Kid, are we going anywhere special or just riding along?"

The Kid looked at me with the biggest grin I'd ever seen on him.

"Oh, it's special, my friend." He began. "You ever heard of the Camel Corps?"

Of course, I shook my head. I had never heard of such a thing. The Kid continued.

"Well, the United States Army brought a bunch of camels in from overseas to use as pack animals.

I guess they thought it was a good idea at the time.

But once the American Civil War ended about ten years ago, there was no more use for the camels. Some were sold, but some just up and wandered off."

The Kid was usually truthful, and although his story sounded pretty crazy, I believed him, and he explained his reasons.

"I've always wanted to see a camel, you know. And not a captured or enslaved one in a circus or a zoo. I've got a hankerin' to see a camel out in the wild."

Well, Avery that sounded like a good idea to me. In the first place, who knew that there were camels running free out there? I sure didn't.

Maybe it was the chance of a lifetime.

We actually did head for the hills, the Black Hills that is, right at the edge of a valley. The Kid said he'd heard the Verde River ran through that valley.

The Kid told me that the camels had been set free not far from where we set up our little camp. Made the most sense that they might be close by.

The trees would shelter us, and there was plenty of water for the horses and us, so it also made the most sense for us to head there.

The Verde River was huge; I think I'd been half expecting some sort of creek.

Anyway, we had water to drink and fish to catch, so we had no worries about starving or dying of thirst."

"What about the horses, grandpa? Horses don't eat fish, do they?" Grandpa laughed a little.

"Oh no, Avery. The horses would graze on the grass – there was grass for as far as the eye could see.

And we brought along a sack of oats to treat them with. Horses love their oats.

So, me and the Kid fished in the morning, did a little hiking during the day, and sat by the campfire at night. We shared stories at the campfire and had a lot of laughs.

I was so relaxed, I'd almost forgotten that we were even looking for the camels. Well, that is until our third night at that camp."

I just about dropped my potato. I grabbed it before it hit the ground, cut it, and tossed the halves into the barrel.

"What happened on the third night?"

"It had been pretty quiet out there in the valley. Nothing but the usual rustle of leaves and the occasional coyote yip or howl.

But on that third night, the coyotes turned up the volume, and we were scared.

So the story goes, they make those noises to communicate with each other, and sometimes even warn of danger.

We were camped in a clearing at a narrow and shallow point of the river, and we agreed it'd be a good idea, if we ran to the trees to hide.

Just as we got up to do that, we heard the heavy pounding of hooves, and the trees on the other side of the river began to sway.

I tripped over a rock and landed on my face.

Well, the Kid was athletic and fast, and in no time, he drug me up by my belt loops and got me back on my feet.

Thinking back, I believe he probably saved my life. No sooner did we get into those trees, the moaning and bellowing began.

We looked on, as the trees on the other side of the river parted, and lo and behold, out lumbered five camels.

They all paced straight to the river to take a long drink.

I looked over at the Kid and saw that he had that big grin on his face again. Well, after all, didn't his dream just come true?"

I nodded. "Did you leave the trees? Did you go pet them or something? What happened?"

I set my knife down, and threw my last two potato halves in the bucket.

"Well, the Kid and I were young, but old enough to know that any wild animal can be unpredictable.

We stood stone still and watched them for a while. But that's not where the story ends."

Just then, grandpa noticed that my potato bowl was empty. He promptly filled it again from his own bowl.

I sighed as I picked up my knife and another potato, then started all over again.

"There was one camel that was different from the others. He wasn't the smallest, nor the biggest in the herd, but he turned out to be more curious than the others.

I guess what made him stand out the most, was his red hair. I didn't know a camel could have red hair, but this one did.

That red camel stood with the rest of his buddies, taking his drink when he stopped suddenly.

We watched as he cocked his head to the side, and listened.

The Kid and I looked at each other, but I have to say, I swear we didn't make a sound.

But something alerted the red camel. Did he sense us? He soon broke free from the rest and waded across that river toward us.

I thought we were goners, Avery. Camels are ordinarily huge beasts, and this one was no different."

"Grandpa, why didn't you run or at least climb a tree? You were in the trees, weren't you?"

"What, and have a whole herd of camels after us? No thanks, Avery. I'd rather take my chances with one.

So, we stood there, me on one side of the tree and the Kid on the other, and braced ourselves for the worst.

That red camel walked straight to us. He lifted his head and sniffed the air and snorted.

And then he leaned his massive head downward and looked me straight in the eye.

Have you ever smelled a camel's breath, Avery?" I shook my head, no.

This time I did drop my potato, but I didn't

bother to pick it up.

"That camel was inches from my face. I guess he was checking me out by my smell. I don't know though, I'm no expert.

We just stood there like that, looking at each other, and breathing heavy; both of us panting, for different reasons. I panted out of pure fright.

It felt like this lasted for hours, but it was probably only minutes.

My worst fear was about to happen. The other camels soon began to follow their friend across the river.

The red camel snorted again, reared up on his hind legs, and then took off downstream.

The other camels followed him. Avery, it was like he was deliberately leading the herd away from us. I felt it in my bones."

"Do... do you think he was protecting you?

Is that what you mean?"

"Kind of, yeah, kind of I do. Well, let me tell you. The Kid and I moved our bedding into the trees and that's where we slept the rest of the night.

The Kid whispered to me, before we finally fell asleep, that he was quite satisfied with having seen five wild camels, and he wanted to ride home the next day.

I couldn't argue with that logic. I think we both thought we got off pretty lucky for having seen those camels, and with no harm done.

So, the next morning, I headed upstream to wash up a bit before we'd get going for home.

The Kid was still snoring, sound asleep."

"Upstream, grandpa? The opposite direction from where the camels had gone, right?" Grandpa nodded.

"That's the one, Avery. I wasn't going to push my luck and run into them again.

So, I was squatting at the river's edge, splashing water on my face, when I heard that familiar snorting.

I slowly got to my feet, and turned around. Right behind me, was that red camel. And he was just kind of looking at me with sad eyes, and snorting softly.

What was I to do? I looked back at him as I stood there, wondering about my fate.

You know what that camel did? He came closer and rubbed his slimy, wet nose on the side of my face."

"Grandpa! Then what did you do?"

"Well, I didn't know what to do. It wasn't like I could yell for help.

I had to think fast, so I remembered what

my mama would do when I was little and sad.

And so, I began to quietly sing a lullaby to that red camel.

We stood together for so long, with me singing and that camel rubbing my face, that I actually went through that same song four times. And Avery, it was not a short song.

The red camel stopped rubbing me with his nose about halfway through my singing to him, and began rubbing my cheek with his.

I've never felt such sharp whiskers in my entire life. But I kept right on singing.

Finally, the red camel gave me one final snort, and lumbered off into the trees.

I wasn't sure how I would ever explain my whisker-rubbed, cheek rash to anyone."

"Did you ever see him again, grandpa?"

"No, I didn't, although I wanted to. Maybe I could have changed the course of history, just a little for the red camel."

"Oh, no! Why, grandpa? You said before that we cannot change history.   What happened to the red camel?"

"Yes, Avery.   We cannot change history when we travel; but in this case, maybe it could have saved a life. We'll never know.

So the story goes, that red camel went on an angry rampage and struck terror into the hearts of a lot of folks.

He became legendary, and was known as the Red Ghost. He even trampled a young woman to death in 1883.

The Red Ghost was finally shot about ten years later by a rancher who found him in his garden."   Grandpa shook his head, and looked a little sad.

"Avery, I will always treasure those moments with the red camel. Wish there was something I could have done for him."

"Grandpa, it doesn't sound like he was full of terror when you met him, though. What happened?"

"Well, any animal can turn mean and nasty if they are mistreated. That's my best guess, Avery.

I'm guessing that my red-haired friend was treated badly, sometime after I met him in 1774."

Our potato bowls were finally both empty, and the barrel was full of halves. I watched as grandpa picked up the barrel and set it in the shade.

"It's still cool enough outside, as long as these stay out of the weather, they'll be fine to plant once that skin forms. Thanks for pitching in, Avery."

Grandpa sat back down on his stump.

"So, back to the Kid. We rode back home over the course of a few days, and we were both rather quiet.

We were happy though, glad to have seen those camels.

About a month later, when the Kid asked me to hop on my horse again and ride for a few days, why wouldn't I?

Once again, we put on our cowboy hats, chaps, and spurs, filled our canteens, saddled our horses and headed west.

How was I to know he'd just escaped from jail for stealing?"

"Grandpa! You were friends with a criminal?" Grandpa chuckled a little.

"I told you, I didn't know. Back then, he would have been called an outlaw, not a criminal.

There was no radio or television back then to announce such things.

The Kid sure didn't tell me. I thought we were just going for a ride.

The Kid carried a pistol on his hip, and he was a very good shot. I'd watch him target practice from time to time.

Guns of any sort, have always made me feel uncomfortable, and so even though I was in the Wild West, I chose not to pack one.

We rode for well over one hundred miles, and it took two full days. It was important for our horses to let them take drinks, eat a bit, and rest. It was a long and dusty ride.

We finally crossed the border and ended up in a little town called Bonita in the State of Arizona."

In my mind, I tried to picture grandpa

riding his horse, long hair and beard flapping in the wind.

"Our canteens had been emptied for a long while, and we were thirsty. We found a saloon and tied our horses up to the rail outside.

Had I known what was about to happen, I would have insisted that we kept on riding to find a whole different saloon."

"Grandpa, what happened?"   I felt goosebumps.

"Well, we took our seats and had our drinks in front of us, when the Kid and some other fellow started arguing.

I wanted to just get up and leave, but the Kid did not.

The arguments got worse, and the name calling began.

The Kid got up and his hand reached for

his gun. The other fellow charged at him and they both tumbled to the floor."

"Grandpa, why didn't you stop him?"

"Nothing I would have liked better, Avery. But, you already know that we cannot alter the course of history.

They grunted and rolled around on that floor, and they fought for the gun. Before I knew what happened, the Kid gut shot him.

The saloon became dead silent. You could have heard a pin drop, it was so quiet.

I stood up from my chair, put my hat on and slowly backed up and out of the saloon.

Then, I just jumped on my horse and hightailed it all the way back to the boarding house in Silver City."

"Did you tell anyone what happened?"

"No, boy. That too, could have changed

history, things yet to come. I just went back to work on the ranch, and minded my own business.

What could I do? The damage had been done."

"What about Henry, the Kid? Did he go back to Silver City, too?"

"I never saw him again. I found out later that the fellow he shot, died the next day.

The Kid was arrested, but I guess he didn't like being locked up very much, and he escaped that jail, too.

He became quite the famous outlaw and sadly, was shot and killed when he was only about twenty-two years old."

Grandpa's eyes got watery and his voice softened.

"I'll always appreciate that friendship, and I wish things could have been different for him.

By the time he died, he didn't use the name, Henry anymore, and he will forever be known as Billy the Kid."

To be continued....

EXTRA READING

The following information is
used with permission by
www.coinsweekly.com

It is not only one of the rarest Islamic gold coins, it is also said to be the most expensive one ever to be sold in an auction. On April 4, 2011, the auction house Morten & Eden sold an Umayyad dinar from 723 AD for £3.7 million (buyer's premium included).

The coin was struck during the reign of Yazid II, the ninth Umayyad caliph. He ruled from 720 to 724. A possible connection of this coin and his haji in 723 has been suggested. According to medieval writers, the caliph purchased territory close to Mecca at the time this coin was minted and a gold mine was located on said territory. This mine "Ma'din Bani Sulaim" (= "Mine of the Commander of the Faithful") is mentioned on the coin. It is the first coin which states a location in its inscription that today is part of the Kingdom of Saudi Arabia.

But, who were the Umayyads?

EXTRA READING
The following information is
used with permission by
islamichistory.org

The Umayyads were the first Muslim dynasty – that is, they were the first rulers of the Islamic Empire to pass down power within their family.

According to tradition, the Umayyad family (also known as the Banu Abd-Shams) and Muhammad (saw) both descended from a common ancestor, Abd Manaf ibn Quasi, and they originally came from the city of Mecca.

Muhammad (saw) descended from Abd Manaf via his son, Hashim, while the Umayyads descended from Abd Manaf via a different son, Abd-Shams, whose son was Umayya.

The two families are therefore considered to be different clans (those of Hashim and of Umayya, respectively) of the same tribe (that of the Quraish).

The shift in power to Damascus, the Umayyad capital city, was to have profound effects on the development of Islamic history.

For one thing, it was a tacit recognition of the end of an era.

The first four caliphs had been without exception Companions of the Prophet – pious, sincere men who had lived no differently from their neighbours and who preserved the simple habits of their ancestors despite the massive influx of wealth from the conquered territories.

Even Uthman, whose policies had such a divisive effect, was essentially dedicated more to the concerns of the next world than of this.

With the shift to Damascus much was changed.

In the early days of Islam, the extension of Islamic rule had been based on an uncomplicated desire to spread the Word of God.

Although the Muslims used force when they met resistance they did not compel their enemies to accept Islam.

On the contrary, the Muslims permitted Christians and Jewish peoples to practice their own faith and numerous conversions to Islam were the result of exposure to a faith that was simple and inspiring.

***

EXTRA READING

The following image and information is
used with permission by
Marshall Trimble, author and Official
Arizona State Historian

Just prior to the outbreak of the Civil War the storied Army Corps of Topographical Engineers used camels as beasts of burden during their survey of a wagon road along the 35th Parallel from Albuquerque to Los Angeles. The camel experiment was highly successful but following the survey the government had no more use for the homely critters and sold some at auction while others were left to roam the deserts of western Arizona. And, therein spawned the legends such as that of the "Red Ghost."

The legend began in 1883 at a lonely ranch at Eagle Creek near the Arizona-New Mexico border when a woman was stomped to death by a strange-looking red-haired beast with a devilish-looking creature strapped on his back.

Then one night a few days later a party of prospectors was awakened to thundering hoofs and terrifying screams stampeding through their camp. Strands of red hair were found clinging to the brush. The Red Ghost attacked again a few days later, this time the monster, described as being 30-tall knocked over two freight wagons. Again, strands of red hair were found in the wreckage. These acts of terror spurred a litany of embellished campfire tales. One claimed he saw it kill a grizzly and eat it. Another said he chased the Red Ghost only to have it disappear before his eyes. All agreed the camel had a human skeleton attached to its back.

Near Phoenix a cowboy came upon the Red Ghost and tossed a loop around its neck only to see the angry beast charge and run right over horse and rider before galloping off in a cloud of dust. The cowboy recognized skeletal remains of a man on its back.

Stories grew to legendary proportions until about a decade later a rancher awoke one morning and saw the Red Ghost grazing in his garden. He drew a bead with his trusty Winchester and dropped the camel with one shot. An examination of the corpse convinced all this was indeed the fabled Red Ghost. The animal's back was badly scarred from rawhide strands that had been used to hold the body of a man. But how the human body came to be attached to the back of a camel remains a cruel mystery.

***

ABOUT THE AUTHOR

The author lives in the beautiful Cowichan Valley on Vancouver Island, British Columbia. She is pleased to present the Coinkeeper Series and she very much looks forward to finding out what's in store for Avery, in the next book.

For more information, please visit:
www.teresaschapansky.com

Manufactured by Amazon.ca
Bolton, ON

18071350R00030